Bill Martin Jr, Ph.D., has devoted his life to the education of young children. Bill Martin Books reflect his philosophy: that children's imaginations are opened up through the play of language, the imagery of illustrations, and the permanent joy of reading books.

Henry Holt and Company, Inc.
Publishers since 1866
115 West 18th Street
New York, New York 10011

Published in Canada by Fitzhenry & Whiteside Ltd.,
195 Allstate Parkway, Markham, Ontario L3R 4T8.
Library of Congress Cataloging-in-Publication Data
Sampson, Michael R.
Star of the circus/by Michael and Mary Beth Sampson;
illustrated by Jose Aruego and Ariane Dewey.
"A Bill Martin Book."
Summary: Each circus animal is pushed off the stage by a
bigger animal until they learn that they all are stars in
the circus.
[1. Circus—Fiction. 2. Animals—Fiction.
3. Competition (Psychology)—Fiction.]
I. Aruego, Jose, ill.
II. Dewey, Ariane, ill. III. Title.
PZ7.S165St 1996 [E]—dc20
96-28806

ISBN 0-8050-4284-9
First Edition—1997
Printed in the
United States of
America on
acid-free paper. ∞
10 9 8 7 6
5 4 3 2 1

MICHAEL & MARY BETH SAMPSON

STAR OF THE CIRCUS

ILLUSTRATED BY
JOSE ARUEGO
& ARIANE DEWEY

A BILL MARTIN BOOK
Henry Holt and Company
New York

"I'm the star of the circus!
I'm the star of the circus!"
said Marvelous Mouse.

"No, you're not!"
said Cannonball Cat.

"I'm the star of the circus!"

"No, you're not!"
said Dazzling Dog.

"I'm the star
of the circus!"

"No, you're not!"
said Crazy Kangaroo.

"I'm the star
    of the circus!"

"No, you're not!"
said Zany Zebra.

"I'm the star
of the circus!"

"No, you're not!"
said Jazzy Giraffe.

"I'm the star of the circus!"

"No, you're not!" said Big Bear.

"I'm the star
of the circus!"

"No, you're not!" said
Elegant Elephant.

"I'm the star
of the circus!"

"No, you're not!"

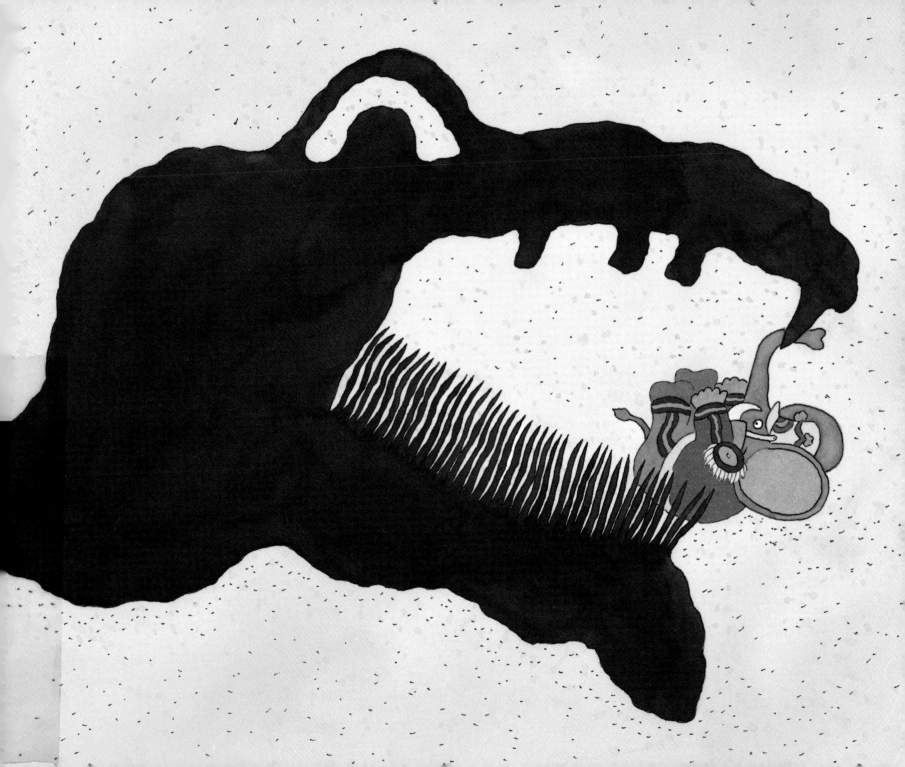

"We're all stars

of the circus!"

To our parents:
Archie and Maurine Glossup
Roy and Ida Sampson.
You will always be stars in our lives.
     —M. S. and M. B. S.

To Juan
  —J. A. and A. D.